Collages were used to prepare the full-color art.
The text type is 28-point Perpetua.

Library of Congress Cataloging-in-Publication Data
Berger, Carin.
Forever friends / by Carin Berger.
p. cm.
"Greenwillow Books."
Summary: In the spring, a blue bird awakens a rabbit and invites him to play,
and they enjoy every day together until it is time for the bird to fly south for
the winter, with a promise to return again next spring.
ISBN 978-0-06-191528-4 (trade bdg.) — ISBN 978-0-06-191529-1 (lib. bdg.)
[1. Friendship—Fiction. 2. Birds—Fiction. 3. Rabbits—Fiction.
4. Seasons—Fiction.] I. Title.
PZ7.B45134For 2010   [E]—dc22   2009018758

10 11 12 13 14 LEO First Edition 10 9 8 7 6 5 4 3 2 1

Greenwillow Books

To friendships that transcend place and time.

To Max and Thea, without whom I could never have managed

this book. And with oceans of gratitude + appreciation to

RV, DD, GG, JK, CL, DR, MR, PR, and PZ.

forever friends

CARIN BERGER

Greenwillow Books
An Imprint of **HarperCollins***Publishers*

149

Winter had ended.
Leaves unfurled and buds blossomed.
High up on a branch
sat a small blue bird.

Snug in a log below slept a little brown bunny.

Hello! Come play! sang the bird,
and the bunny did.

Soon they were friends.

They played all spring . . .

and summer . . .

right through till late fall.

Now I must fly south, said the bird.

But I promise, come spring, I'll be back.

The forest felt
cold and lonely.
The bunny missed
the bird.

The bird missed the bunny, too.

December . . . January . . . February.

At last,   the sun

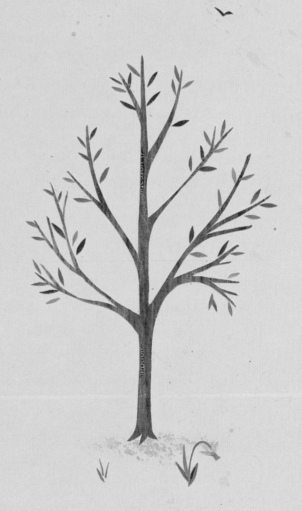

chased away

the snow.

Spring had come once more.

One morning, after waiting so long,
the bunny awoke to the most wonderful song.

Come play, come play, sang the bird.
And, with a leap of joy, the bunny did.

They were forever friends.